Words to Know Before You Read

amazing

explained

fluffernutter

grumbled

halftime

happily

menu

marshmallow

proudly

wrap

www.rourkepublishing.com

Edited by Luana K. Mitten
Illustrated by Helen Poole
Art Direction and Page Layout by Renee Brady

Library of Congress Cataloging-in-Publication Data

Picou, Lin
 Do I Have To... / Lin Picou.
    p. cm. -- (Little Birdie Books)
 ISBN 978-1-61741-816-7 (hard cover) (alk. paper)
 ISBN 978-1-61236-020-1 (soft cover)
 Library of Congress Control Number: 2011924693

Rourke Publishing
Printed in China, Voion Industry
   Guangdong Province
042011
042011LP

www.rourkepublishing.com - rourke@rourkepublishing.com
Post Office Box 643328 Vero Beach, Florida 32964

Do I Have To...

By Lin Picou

Illustrated by Helen Poole

"Jacob, please take out the trash?"

"Do I have to?" Jacob asked. "I'm busy."

"Mom, I'm hungry. Will you fix me lunch?"

"Do I have to? I'm busy," said Mom.

"But Mom, you said I needed to eat lunch before Sarah's birthday party," Jacob explained.

"You're right. Why don't you make lunch?"
Mom asked.

"Dad, will you take me to Sarah's birthday party after lunch?"

"Do I have to? I'm busy watching a football game," Dad grumbled.

Oh no, thought Jacob. How can I get Mom and Dad to help?

"Mom, if I make lunch for you and Dad, will you help me wrap Sarah's present?" Jacob asked.

Mom happily agreed.

"Dad," Jacob asked. "If I fix you lunch, will you drive me to the party?"

"Yes," agreed Dad. "Let's go during halftime."

In minutes, Jacob had made three sandwiches and his Mom had filled three glasses with milk.

"Sweet!"

"What's on the menu?" Dad asked.

"Fluffernutter sandwiches!" Jacob answered proudly. "I used marshmallow fluff and peanut butter."

"Amazing!"

Then Mom and Jacob wrapped Sarah's present while Dad found his car keys.

Mom said, "We make a wonderful team when we help each other!"

After Reading Activities

You and the Story...

What did Jacob want his parents to do?

How did Jacob get his parents to help him?

Have you ever helped someone with something to get them to help you? What did you do?

Words You Know Now...

Several of the words below have added endings. Choose three words with added endings (ing, ed, ly). Write each word without its ending. Does that change the meaning of the word?

amazing	happily
explained	marshmallow
fluffernutter	menu
grumbled	proudly
halftime	wrap

You Could...Plan a Lunch for Your Parents or Family Members

- Decide what you will fix for lunch for your family.

- Make a list of all of the ingredients you will need to make lunch.

- Be sure to set the table with everything you will need (plates, silverware, glasses, salt and pepper.)

- Invite your parents or family members to your special lunch.

- Enjoy this special time with your family.

About the Author

Lin Picou teaches in Lutz, Florida. Her students practice following directions and math skills when they make fun foods like Dirt Pudding and Jell-O Aquariums for their snacking pleasure.

About the Illustrator

Helen Poole lives in Liverpool, England, with her fiancé. Over the past ten years she has worked as a Designer and Illustrator on books, toys, and games for many stores and publishers worldwide. Her favorite part of illustrating is character development. She loves creating fun, whimsical worlds with bright, vibrant colors.

She gets her inspiration from everyday life and has her sketchbook with her at all times as inspiration often strikes in the unlikeliest of places!